Winnie AND Wilbur
The Santa Surprise

To Ellie Payton with love. K.P.
For Father Christmas, because he deserves treats, too. xx

OXFORD
UNIVERSITY PRESS

Great Clarendon Street, Oxford OX2 6DP
Oxford University Press is a department of the University of Oxford.
It furthers the University's objective of excellence in research, scholarship,
and education by publishing worldwide. Oxford is a registered trade mark
of Oxford University Press in the UK and in certain other countries

First published 2018

First published in paperback 2019

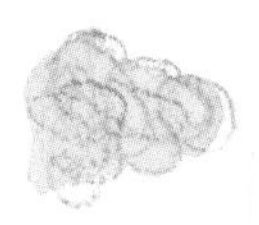

British Library Cataloguing in Publication Data

Data available

ISBN 978-0-19-276746-2

1 3 5 7 9 10 8 6 4 2

Printed in China

Paper used in the production of this book is a natural,
recyclable product made from wood grown in sustainable forests.
The manufacturing process conforms to the environmental
regulations of the country of origin.

Winnie AND Wilbur
The Santa Surprise

LAURA OWEN KORKY PAUL

CONTENTS

CHAPTER 1
COUNTING DOWN TO CHRISTMAS

CHAPTER 2
PERFECT PLANS FOR PRESENTS

CHAPTER 3
MORE KNOTS THAN KNITTING

CHAPTER 4
WRAPPED AND READY (THEN RIPPED)

CHAPTER 5
A BARGAIN BEAR

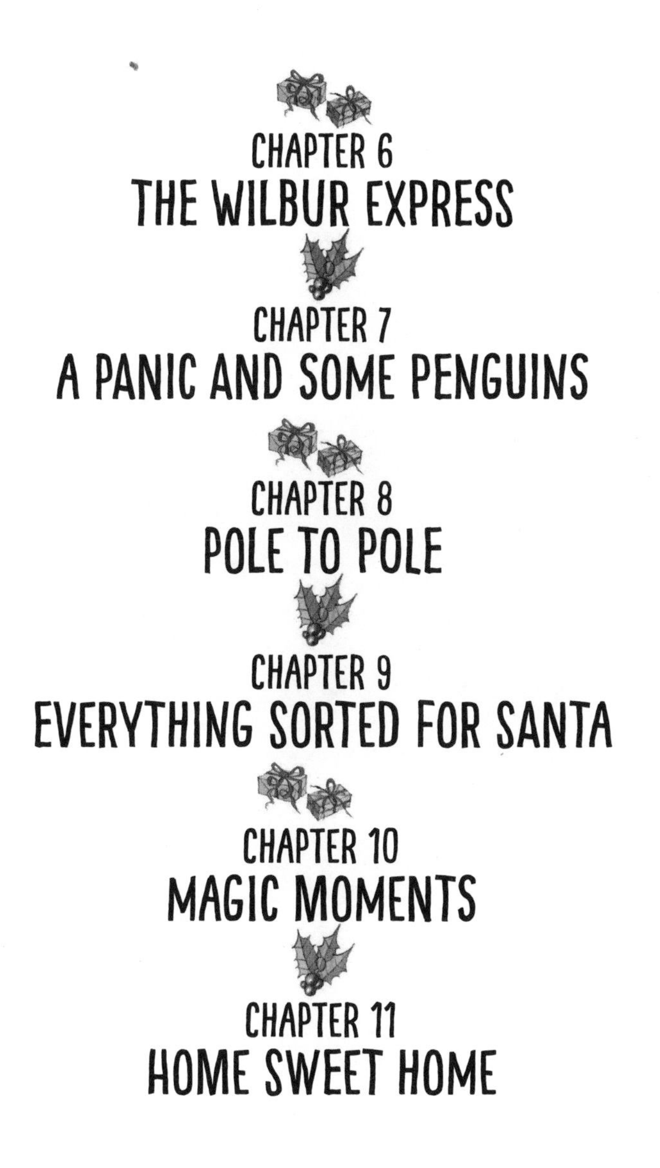

CHAPTER 6
THE WILBUR EXPRESS

CHAPTER 7
A PANIC AND SOME PENGUINS

CHAPTER 8
POLE TO POLE

CHAPTER 9
EVERYTHING SORTED FOR SANTA

CHAPTER 10
MAGIC MOMENTS

CHAPTER 11
HOME SWEET HOME

CHAPTER 1

COUNTING DOWN TO CHRISTMAS

'My turn!' said Winnie, leaping out of bed, tangling her feet in her nightie, and falling onto the floor.

Splat!

Wilbur had their advent calendar in one paw. He was just teasing open the corner of a door.

'Hey, you opened yesterday's door!' said Winnie. 'It's my turn today. Give it to me!' Winnie paused. 'Hey, Wilbur,

why don't you guess what the picture is behind the calendar door? If you get it right, I'll let you open the next two doors. Go on, Wilbur, guess!'

Wilbur put a claw to his chin and frowned. Then he smiled and drew on the misty window.

'Is that a fish in a dish?' said Winnie. 'That's not very Christmassy. I think it's going to be a picture of ding-dong-sing-along Christmas bells and singers,' said Winnie.

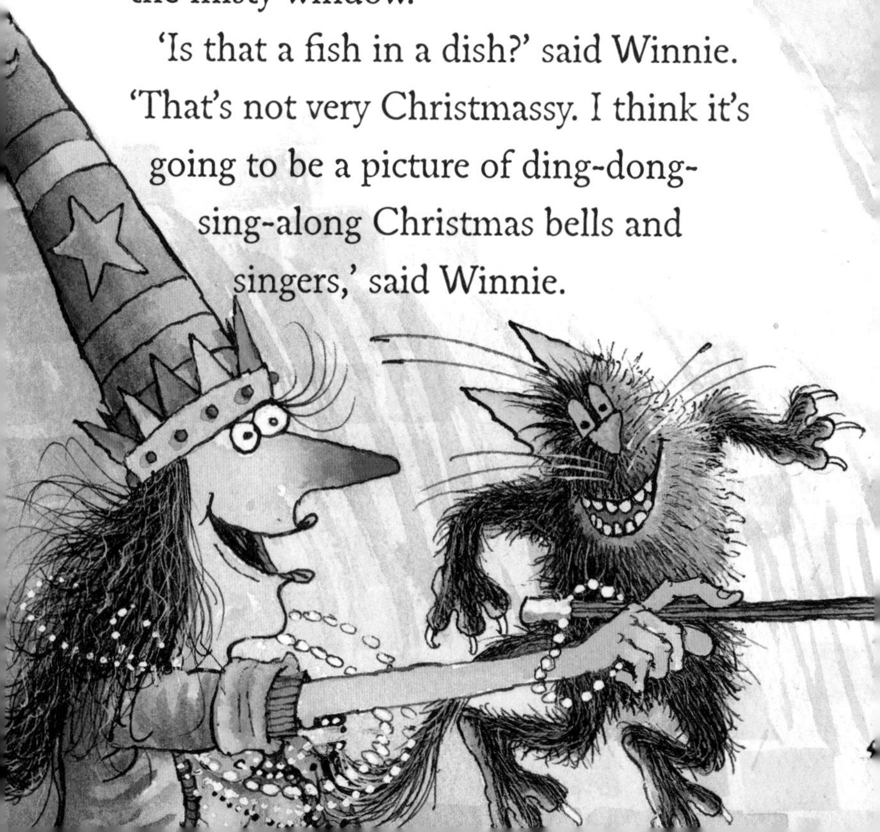

She carefully opened the calendar door. 'Look, Wilbur! A lovely pile of PRESENTS! We were both wrong! Oo, but what are we doing about presents this year? What shall we give and what shall we ask Santa for?' A dreamy look came over Wilbur's face.

'Let's do our letters to Santa now,' said Winnie. Winnie waved her wand over the table. '**Abracadabra!**' There was a pile of paper and crayons and pencils and glitter and glue.

Winnie wasn't good at writing, but she could draw, so she did a bit of both. 'Deer Santa pleez can I hav . . .' She chewed on a pencil, thinking for a few moments, then she drew some bat hair clips, some wand candy canes, a bag of eyeball marbles, and a jigsaw puzzle that had 1013 pieces.

Wilbur drew something too. It was a rectangle.

'What's that, Wilbur?' said Winnie. 'It looks as dull as snail porridge with no nit sprinkles to stir into it.'

Wilbur pointed at a page in a shiny magazine that had come through the door. It said, 'Get your claws on the new PawTech tablet. Comes with free cat strap for easy carrying.'

'It still looks as boring as slug snoring to me,' said Winnie. 'How about if I get you one of those things now, then you can ask Santa for something more Christmassy?'

Winnie waved her wand over the picture in the catalogue.

'Abracadabra!'

Instantly, Wilbur's new PawTech was on the table.

'Meowowsy-wowsy!' said Wilbur, and he began to tap and swipe the screen. He was making a great long list of present ideas.

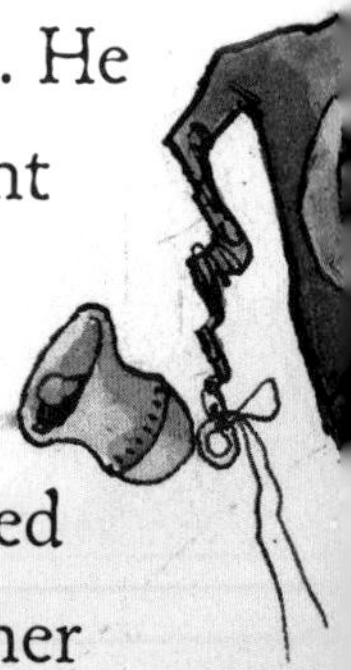

'Oo, that thing's more interesting than I'd thought it would be,' admitted Winnie. She was gluing glitter onto her letter . . . and on to herself and on to Wilbur. 'I'm making my letter pretty because Santa works so hard bringing everybody presents, and he deserves . . .' Winnie stopped still, glue stick in the air. 'Oh, Wilbur, I've just had a thought that's as big as a hairy mammoth! What about Santa?'

'Meow?' asked Wilbur.

Winnie opened her arms and hands. 'Wilbur, WHO GIVES SANTA PRESENTS?'

'Mruh-oh,' said Wilbur. He'd never thought about that.

'Does *anybody* give Santa presents?' said Winnie. 'Proper presents that are more than a drinkie and squince pie?'

Wilbur shook his head. He didn't think that anybody *did* give Santa proper surprise sort of presents.

'Well, that's as not fair as a snail getting boots for his birthday,' said Winnie. 'It's actually worse than that because at least the snail has something to unwrap. Oh, Wilbur.'

Paaarp!

Winnie blew her nose. 'It's so sad to think of poor Santa hanging his stocking every year, and every Christmas morning finding it still empty. And after he has filled gazillions of other stockings with presents!'

Winnie pushed aside her letter to Santa. 'Right,' she

said. 'What we need is a plan. You and I must take presents to Santa, Wilbur. You can make the plan on that tablet thingy of yours.'

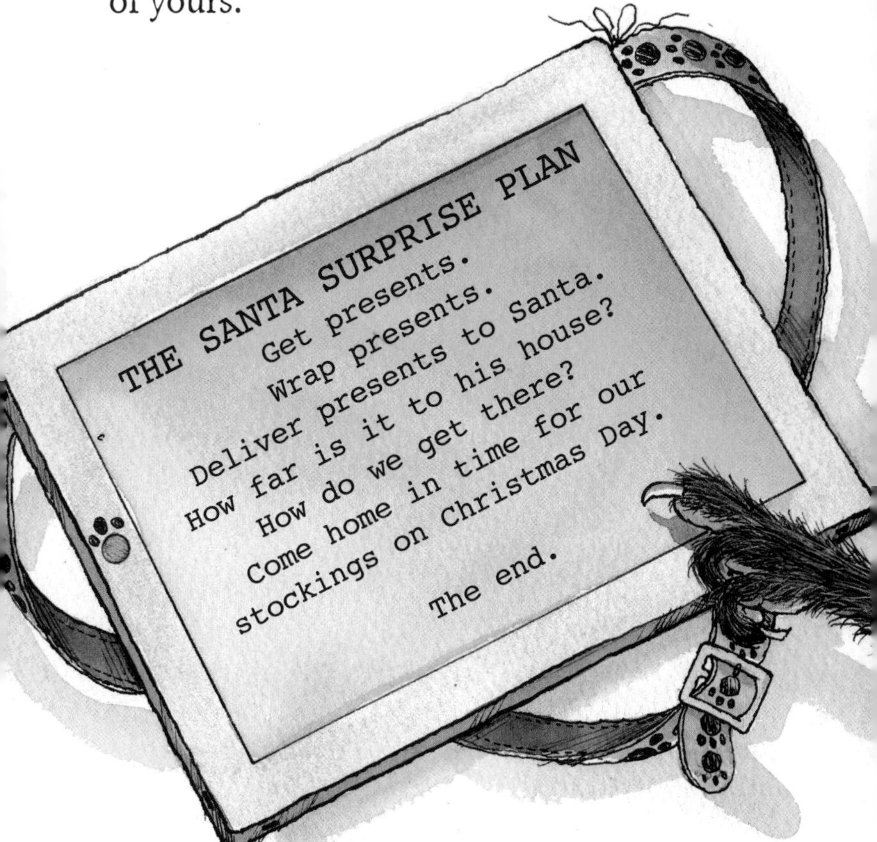

'Now we need a list of the presents to get for him,' said Winnie. 'Write down "chocolate elves," Wilbur. And "a new belt"—because I bet his tummy grows after eating all those squincy pies!' Then she frowned. 'But what else would Santa like, do you think? A beard comb?'

Wilbur did a thumbs down to that idea.

'Too hurty in the tangles?' said Winnie. 'You're probably right. What, then? I'm sure those little ordinaries at the school would have present ideas as good as a Christmas pud. Shall we go and ask them?'

Wilbur nodded enthusiastically.

'Righto. I'll get my broomstick and we can go,' said Winnie.

CHAPTER 2

PERFECT PLANS FOR PRESENTS

The school looked lovely and Christmassy. Winnie and Wilbur were hurrying to find the little ordinaries when they bumped into the head teacher.

'Excuse me just one mini-maggoty-moment, Mr Head Teacher,' said Winnie. 'You're an old man like Santa, so what do you think Santa would like for Christmas?'

'Erm, perhaps a new pencil sharpener,' said the head teacher. Winnie made her tasting-lemon-juice face.

'A pencil sharpener?' she said. 'That's too snoringly boring!'

'A new tie, then?' said the head teacher. 'A green tweed one would be most acceptable as a present.'

'Does Santa ever even wear ties?' asked Winnie. 'Is there one under his red jacket? I don't think so. And when it's not Christmas, Santa might wear shorts and flip-flops at home. Or swishy robes. Or even a dress? None of those would go with a tie. He might even wear nothing at all!'

'Oh, really!' said the head teacher and flounced off.

'I think your idea to give presents to Santa is wonderful, Winnie!' said Mrs Parmar, the school secretary. 'I'd like to make some suggestions. He's given me so many presents over the years and it would be nice to return the favour.'

'What do you think we should give him, then?' said Winnie.

'I think that the best presents are home-made ones,' said Mrs Parmar. 'Then you know they've been made just for you. Why don't you knit something for Santa?'

'Er, because my knitting always comes out in a knitted-knotted mess,' said Winnie.

'I could teach you how to knit better, if you like?' said Mrs Parmar. She was in such a Christmassy mood that she had forgotten that doing things with Winnie always seemed to end up very differently from what she had intended. 'You could knit Santa a nice pair of socks,' said Mrs Parmar. 'Men like socks. Socks or biscuits.'

'Ooh yes, I am better at baking than knitting!' said Winnie. 'How about a cobweb-snowflake cake with beetle crunch and candied spiders?'

'Er, well, um, maybe Santa would like something a bit less *original* than one of your recipes?' said Mrs Parmar. 'A gingerbread house would be Christmassy.' So they added that to the list.

The children had LOTS of ideas. The list on Wilbur's tablet grew.

'A reindeer space hopper so that Santa can jump from roof to roof.'

'Sparkly bubble bath for when he gets home from flying around the world.'

'Earphones to let him listen to Christmas music as he flies.'

'A Christmas Joke book!'

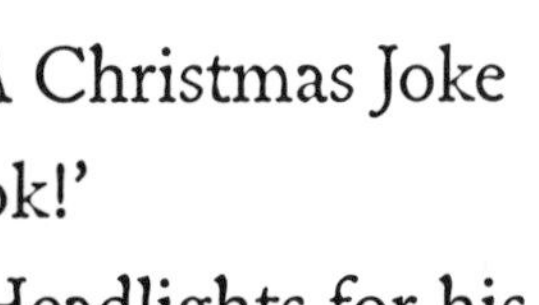

'Headlights for his sleigh.'

'Binoculars with antlers.'

'A football that looks like a Christmas pudding!'

'Mittens that look like kitten paws.'

'All brillaramaroodles ideas!' said Winnie. 'We'll get every one of them for Santa. Bye!'

Just as Winnie and Wilbur were going out of the school door, a little girl tugged at Winnie's dress.

'Please,' she said, 'will you give my Teddums to Santa? Teddums is my Best Thing.'

'Are you sure you want to give Teddums away?' said Winnie. 'Wilbur's my Best

Thing. But I'd never give him to Santa!'

'Meow,' said Wilbur.

'I am sure,' said the girl, and she handed Teddums to Winnie.

'You are as kind as a kangaroo that gives free rides in its pocket,' Winnie told her. 'Thank you.'

CHAPTER 3
MORE KNOTS THAN KNITTING

Mrs Parmar flew home with Winnie and Wilbur.

'Oo, my goodness!' she said, straightening her hair when they landed. 'I think I rather like flying!' Then she wagged a finger at Winnie. 'It's time you got knitting if you're going to make Santa's socks in time for Christmas.' Then she raised an eyebrow at Wilbur, 'And you, I think, need to do something

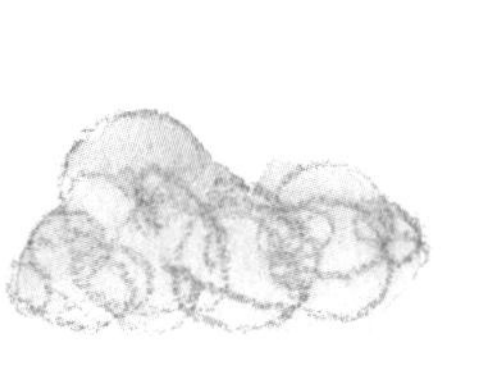

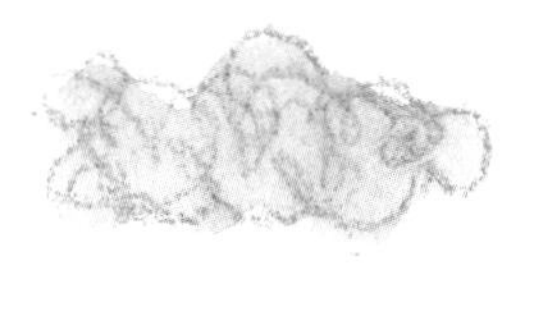

about a sledge for taking all the presents to the North Pole.'

Wilbur set to work with logs and sticks from the wood pile, and a hammer and nails.

Inside the house, Mrs Parmar tried to explain knitting to Winnie, but Winnie wasn't listening properly.

'Oh, I know, I know!' said Winnie. 'You poke sticks into the wool, flick them about a bit, and a sock grows on the sticks. Is that right?'

'Er, not quite,' said Mrs Parmar.

'You need to . . .' But Winnie was already frantically working at a tangle of wool with her wand and a wooden spoon. 'Oh, I'll leave you to it,' sighed Mrs Parmar. 'I'll get making that gingerbread.'

Mrs Parmar mixed butter and sugar and flour and spices. She kneaded and rolled and cut.

'Aren't you going to add some dried ants to it to give it a nice crunch?' said Winnie.

'No, I am not!' said Mrs Parmar.

'Or red beetles to make it nice and holly-spotty?'

'No.'

'Or . . .'

'I'm quite sure that Santa would like his gingerbread to taste of just gingerbread and icing,' said Mrs Parmar firmly. Her cooking did smell wonderfully spicy when she took the trays out of the oven.

'My knitting's not going very well,'

admitted Winnie. She held up the knotty mess. 'It looks more like a fishing net that sharks have escaped from than a sock. And I wanted to give Santa a really nice present!'

Mrs Parmar felt sorry for Winnie. She took a deep breath. 'Would you like to fit my gingerbread pieces together to make a house?'

'Yippeee, yes please!' said Winnie, flinging her knitting aside. 'Let's make it just like my house.'

They mixed slurpy-sloppy icing, and splodged it into a nozzled bag for squirting. Mrs Parmar had brought sweets ('No candied weevils or frosted fungus,' she insisted), and they stuck the gingerbread together and decorated it all over.

'Magnifaramaroodles!' said Winnie who was now stuck together with icing and decorated all over, too.

'It does look surprisingly good!' agreed Mrs Parmar.

Just then, there was a *ding-dong-boo-hoo!*

'What in the world is that peculiar noise?' said Mrs Parmar.

'It's somebody at the door,' said Winnie. 'But I've never heard my dooryell crying before.'

When Winnie opened the door, she saw the girl from the school on the doorstep. She was sobbing.

'Whatever is the matter with you?' said Winnie.

'I . . . *gulp* . . . don't . . . *sniff* . . . want

13
Creak!
ΠΡΕΣ

Santa to have my Best Thing Teddums after all!' she wailed. 'I want my Teddums ba-a-a-ck!'

'Oh!' said Winnie. 'Come inside, little ordinary, and we'll find your teddy for you.' Winnie found Teddums in the pile of presents for Santa. The girl clutched him tight, but she went on crying. 'Whatever's the matter now?' said Winnie.

'I'm . . . *sob* . . . still sad . . . *sniff* . . . for Sa-a-a-anta!' she wailed. 'I want him to have a teddy too-oo-oo!'

'Please don't worry, I promise we'll make sure Santa gets a teddy. Here, have a mixing spoon to lickety-lick.'

The little girl stopped sobbing and Mrs Parmar took her and her Teddums home.

CHAPTER 4
WRAPPED AND READY (THEN RIPPED)

'Your sledge is splendiferous,' Winnie told Wilbur. 'But my socks for Santa

are a messy muddle. They're more for scrubbing pans with than wearing. Mrs P did say that men *particularly* like socks for Christmas and I don't want to disappoint Santa. What shall I do?'

Wilbur stood on tiptoe and held a paw up high.

'Meow?' he suggested.

'Well, that's an idea! Maybe Jerry does have some spare socks?' said Winnie.

Jerry, the giant who lived next door to Winnie, was very happy to give some of his socks to Santa.

'I loves Santa, I do,' he told Winnie and Wilbur as he looked under his bed and found two socks, one with pink and green stripes and one green with pink spots. 'They're very almost clean, and sort of slightly a pair,' he said. Scruff, Jerry's dog, loved Santa too. He gave Wilbur and Winnie a bone for Santa.

'Oh! Er, I'm not sure that San . . .' began Winnie.

'Meow!' said Wilbur firmly, so Winnie took the bone too.

They carried the gigantic socks and the bone back to Winnie's house.

'Now we need to magic all the lovely ideas that the little ordinaries thought of into presents,' said Winnie. 'Where's the list on that gadget of yours, Wilbur?' Winnie pulled her wand out of her knitting, then she waved it over Wilbur's PawTech, this way, that way, over there, and back again. '**Abracadabra!**' she said.

And suddenly all the presents appeared, in a big pile.

'I might as well use that knotted wool for making something for Santa's elves, don't you think?' said Winnie, and she waved her wand over the woolly mess,

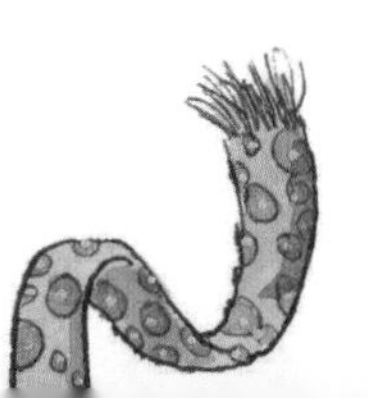

'Abracadabra!'

In a colourful whirlwind of wool and clackety needles, small scarf after small scarf grew, then dropped off the needles, each one of them different.

'Like warm woolly caterpillars!' said Winnie. 'Now we're ready to wrap everything up. Isn't this exciting!' She waved her wand over the pile of presents.

'Abracadabra!'

Swish-crackle-wrap!

'There!' said Winnie. 'Everything wrapped and ready. Wilbur? Wilbur!'

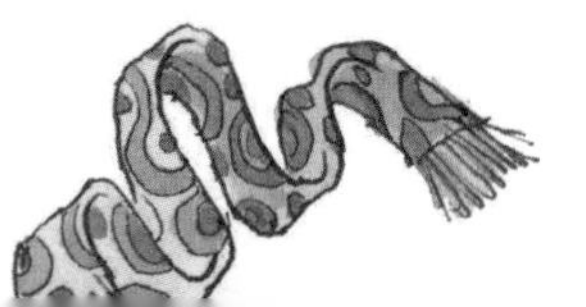

'Mrrow!' said a very cross parcel with a big spotty bow.

'Oh, whoopsy!' said Winnie, and she ripped Wilbur out of his wrapping.

'Meow-meow-meow!' said Wilbur. Then he put his paws up behind his head like teddy bear ears.

'Oh, of course,' said Winnie. 'I promised the little ordinary that Santa would have a teddy. Do you think I could knit one?'

'Meeeeo-noooooo!'

'Well, my poor wand is drooping and pooped after so much magic all at once. It's as exhausted as a tired exhaust pipe,' said Winnie. 'I think this time we'd better just go and buy a teddy bear from a shop like ordinary people do.' Winnie did a little skip. 'And it will be a treat to see the Christmas lights and hear the Christmas music and everything!'

CHAPTER 5
A BARGAIN BEAR

Weeeeeee!

Winnie and Wilbur flew over woods and rooftops.

'Look!' pointed Winnie. 'An enormaroodles shop! That's bound to have a whole lot of teddy bears.'

They parked the broomstick and went inside.

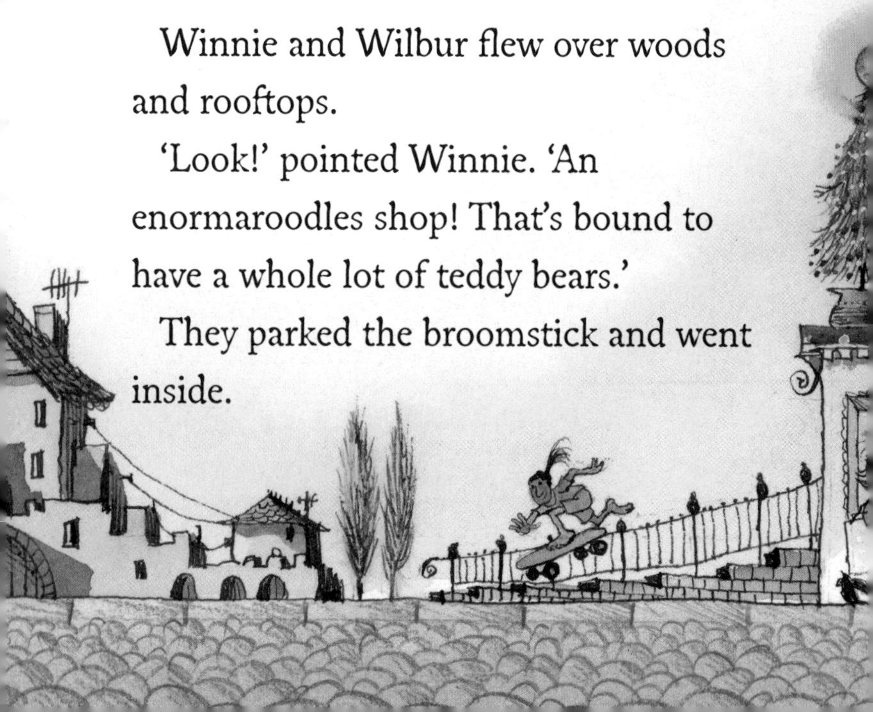

13

'Wowsy!' said Winnie. 'There's so much sparkle and stuff everywhere. How in the world do we find a teddy bear?'

Wilbur led the way.

The toy department was noisy and busy, with toys piled high all around.

'Oh, look at this teddy bear,' said Winnie, stroking the soft fur of a great big bear. 'Let's get this one for Santa!'

'Meow!' said Wilbur, pointing at the price label.

'Oh, my goodness-Christmas-pudness, we can't afford that. Er, how much money have we got, exactly?' Winnie turned out her pockets and three little coins fell onto the floor.

'Are there any bears that only cost that much?' she said.

Wilbur pointed to a very tiny white polar bear. 'That's too small for a big person like Santa,' said Winnie. But Wilbur took the tiny bear and the coins to the till and bought it.

Winnie looked into the paper bag. 'It's as sweet as a gobslopper sweetie, but it's so teensy small you couldn't cuddle it at all, and that's the whole point of a teddy. I know what, I'll make it bigger!' Winnie whipped out her wand.

'Meow!' warned Wilbur, but Winnie wasn't listening.

Winnie waved her wand over the bear in the bag, and '**Abracadabra!**'

Rip! Grrrrrrrrrowl!
13

'A bear!' 'Help!' 'Run for your lives!'

'Quick, Wilbur, hide in here with me!' said Winnie.

Soon the toy shop floor was empty, except for a scowling polar bear. Huge and white, it prowled around, knocking over tables and sniffing the ground. Wilbur was busy filming the polar bear on his PawTech. Then Winnie and Wilbur both jumped in the air because . . .

'Oh, Wilbur, the big bear is crying!' whispered Winnie.

Boo hoo!

'Meow!' went Wilbur as the polar bear's big black nose almost sucked him up like a vacuum cleaner.

'Oi, give me my Wilbur back!' shouted Winnie, jumping out from her hiding place.

'I just want someone to love me,' said the polar bear. 'I'm so far away from my family. And nobody here likes me!'

'Oh, don't cry!' said Winnie, pulling out a hankie to wipe the bear's tears. 'Wilbur and I like you! After all, we did buy you, so that proves we like you and want you!'

'But you ran away from me after you made me real.' More tears ran down the bear's furry face. 'I'm lonely and I just want to go home!'

'Come home with Wilbur and me,' said Winnie.

'Meow?!' said Wilbur.

'Our house is big enough for all of us,'

said Winnie. 'What's your name, bear?'

'Nanoq,' said the bear.

'Well, I'm Winnie and this is Wilbur. So now we're all friends.'

A polar bear is an exceptionally heavy passenger for a broomstick. Nanoq was even heavier than Mrs Parmar!

The broomstick could not lift Winnie and Wilbur *and* Nanoq into the air until Winnie waved her wand.

'Abracadabra!'

Then they wobbled skywards and homewards, where they landed with a bump!

'Well done, Broomy,' said Winnie.

It was a *squeeze* to get Nanoq through the front door, but with Winnie pulling and Wilbur pushing, at last she was through and into Winnie's house.

Pop!

'I'll make this into a nice ice room for you, Nanoq,' said Winnie, waving her wand. '**Abracadabra!**' Instantly, the walls and floor were as icy as a freezer.

Splat!

Wilbur slipped over on the ice as he brought some of his frozen fish to share with Nanoq. 'Mrrow!'

Nanoq smiled a small smile at last.

'We need ice skates, Wilbur,' said Winnie. She waved her wand again and in moments she and Wilbur, and Nanoq too, were all swishing and swooshing all over the room.

Wheeeeee!

Then suddenly Nanoq sat down on the ice. Her mouth had gone from curvy up to curvy down.

'Oh Nanoq, what's wrong?' said Winnie.

'I miss being on the ice with my family,' said Nanoq. 'Please can you take me home?'

'Where is your home?' asked Winnie.

Wilbur pointed at the advent calendar picture of Santa's house at the North Pole.

'Oh! Well that's as perfect as pickled pumpkin!' said Winnie. 'Wilbur and I are going there to take Santa his presents, so you can come with us!'

Nanoq smiled such a big smile this time that she showed her large glinty-sharp teeth. (Which made Winnie and

Wilbur a little bit nervous and quite glad that they were taking her home.)

But *how* exactly would they take Nanoq home? Winnie's broomstick had struggled just bringing her back from the shop. How could a whole pile of presents fit as well, and for such a long journey?

Winnie decided they all needed to sleep on it.

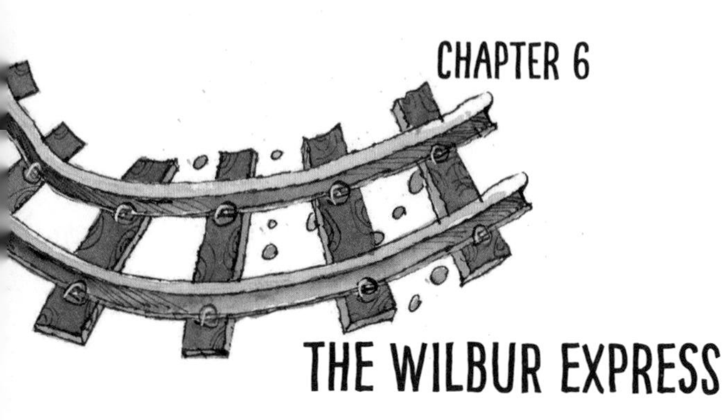

CHAPTER 6

THE WILBUR EXPRESS

Wilbur reached out a paw to the advent calendar. By now, most of the doors were already open.

'Oh, wibble-wobbles, we need to get a squiggle on if we're going to get the presents to Santa before he flies off on Christmas Eve,' said Winnie.

Wilbur showed Winnie the picture behind the new door: it was a train.

'Oo, that's given me a clever-as-a-tap-dancing octopus idea!' said Winnie. 'We'll make a train to take us and everything to Santa's place!'

'Meow?' said Wilbur.

'Well, you remember what that Fairy Godmother did with pumpkins and rats? I'm going to make a flying train out of your sledge and my broomstick and any vegetables we've got in the fridge. Come outside, Wilbur, and help me line everything up.'

Wilbur gave that idea a claws up.

They got everything in place. Then Winnie waved her wand.

'Abracadabra!'

And suddenly there was the train as well as the tracks for it to take off from.

'Help me load it up!' said Winnie. They piled all the presents into the cargo containers. Nanoq settled herself in another compartment, with fish sweets to suck in case she felt travel sick on the journey.

'You can sit next to me at the front, Wilbur,' said Winnie, 'and help me drive. Have you got a map?'

Wilbur swiped his PawTech, and a map appeared. Winnie bent right over to looked closely at the map.

'Okey-pokey, hold tight everyone, I know which way to go.' She pulled the whistle cord and they sped down the track, faster and faster . . . until they took off, up into the sky!

Woo-woo! Choo-choo!

'Yaaaaay!' said Winnie.

'Meow!' said Wilbur.

Nanoq felt a bit sick. So she sucked on her fish sweet.

'Oh, woopsy-doopsy!' said Winnie as the space hopper and the chocolates

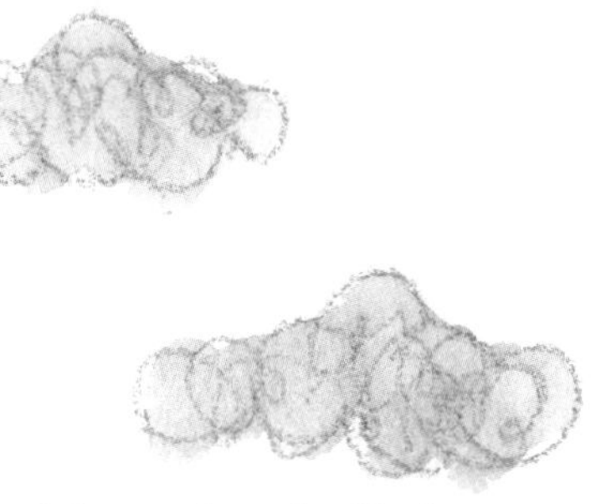

and the Christmas pudding football flew off the train. But most of the presents stayed in place.

Chuntera-whoosh!

They sped through the sky, lumpity-bumping through clouds, sometimes seeing land below, then sea, then more land.

'The land's getting whiter!' said Winnie.

Clackety-clack!

Wilbur's teeth chattered, because it was getting colder too.

'Oh dear, oh dear,' said Nanoq, who couldn't bear to look at all. 'Are we nearly there yet?'

13A
13

'Yup in a cocoa cup, we are!' said Winnie. 'Hold on tight, everyone, we're coming down to land.' The train slowed as it came down through the sky to land softly, with a *flump-flump-flump* of carriages, into the snow below.

Winnie, Wilbur, and Nanoq stepped off and stared into the whiteness.

'Right, now, where is Santa's house?' wondered Winnie.

'And where are the other bears?' said Nanoq.

'Meow,' said Wilbur, looking all around and shaking his head.

All they could see in any direction was ice and snow.

'Oh,' said Winnie. 'Blooming bloomers, now what do we do?'

Clackety-clack went Wilbur's teeth.

A large polar bear tear dropped from Nanoq's eye and made a hole in the snow. 'Oh dear, oh dear,' she sniffed.

'Where, oh where, is Santa?' said Winnie.

CHAPTER 7

A PANIC AND SOME PENGUINS

'You and I can wear some woollies from the presents for Santa, Wilbur,' said Winnie, jumping about to try and get warm. 'I expect Santa has plenty of winter clothes, so he probably won't miss them. Can you find the right packages?' They pulled on gloves and scarves.

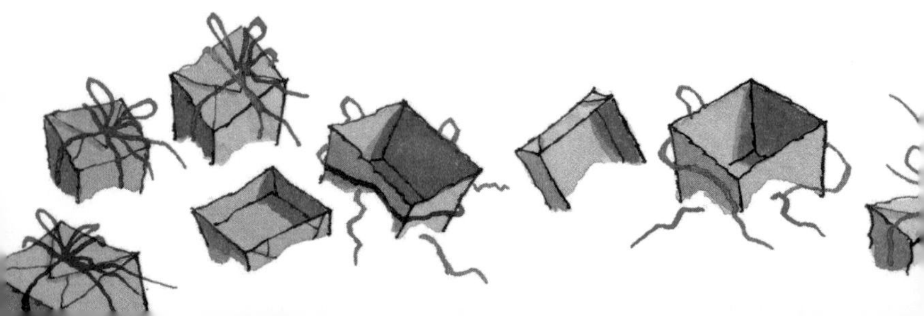

'Oo, I can think a bit better now that I'm warmer,' said Winnie. 'Nanoq, you're the highest of us. Can *you* see Santa or any polar bears? The bears might be hard to see against the white snow.'

Nanoq stood up as
high as she could, which was
very high, and she looked all around.
'Nobody there,' she said.
'Let's use the binoculars,' said Winnie,
tearing open another parcel. She lifted the
binoculars to look and see . . .
'Oo, oo, I can see Santa! At least, er, there
is somebody moving, and it's not a white
somebody so it can't be a polar bear.'
Sniff! Plop!
'Don't cry, Nanoq,' said
Winnie.

'I'm sure we'll find your family soon.'

Wilbur held his PawTech out to Winnie. On it was a picture of Santa.

'Yes, Wilbur, I know Santa is usually dressed in red. But today he's wearing a long black jacket and a white shirt. I wonder why he's doing that wobbly walk? Let's go and ask him, and give him his presents.'

At that moment, midnight struck on Winnie's witch-watch, and the train turned back into the broomstick and sledge.

'Oh, good,' said Winnie. 'We need a sledge, Wilbur, for the snow. I'll just adapt my broomstick.' She waved her wand. '**Abracadabra!**' And suddenly the broomstick was a ski-doodle-doo with the sledge attached behind it. 'Hop on board, Wilbur,' said Winnie. 'Nanoq, you'll just have to run. We're coming, Santa!'

They shot off across the snow, and were rushing towards the black and white figure, when there was a loud

Splosh!

'Oh, no! Where did he go?' said Winnie. 'Not into the icy water? He'll be as frozen as a fish finger that's forgotten to wear gloves!'

Swoosh!

'Meow,' said Wilbur, tapping Winnie on the shoulder, then pointing.

'Oh, my galloping goodness!' said Winnie. 'I can see lots of Santas. Oo, this is very confusing!'

More and more black and white figures waddled across the ice towards

Winnie and Wilbur and Nanoq.

'Oh! I never knew Santa had a beak!' said Winnie.

Wilbur tapped his PawTech to show Winnie a picture of a penguin.

'Oh!' said Winnie. 'Not Santa, after all!'

Up popped the penguin that had dived into the water.

'Pswississ,' whispered Wilbur into Winnie's ear.

'Good idea, that cat!' said Winnie. 'These penguins might know where Santa is. If we're nice to them, they'll help us, won't they? Besides, everybody should get presents at Christmas. Let's give them an elf scarf parcel each. Happy Christmas, you penguins!'

The penguins liked their scarves. A kind little penguin in a spotty scarf even brought them a present of some fish, which made Wilbur and Nanoq happy. But Winnie wasn't happy.

When she asked the penguins where Santa was, they just shook their beaks and shrugged their wings.

'So wherever in this freeze-your-nose place can Santa have got to?' said Winnie. She suddenly yawned so wide you could see right inside her mouth. 'I'm as tired as a wheel on a bus, I am. It's the middle of the night, and no one has switched the sun off!' She rubbed her eyes. 'Well, I need some bo-bos, which means that I need a bed in a house.'

She started ripping more of Santa's presents, looking for the gingerbread house.

'Perfect!' said Winnie when she found it. 'Stand back all you bears and birdies and cats!' She waved her wand. **'Abracadabra!'** And, instantly, the gingerbread house was big enough to fit a witch and a cat and a bear inside. The penguins settled down in snow hollows outside.

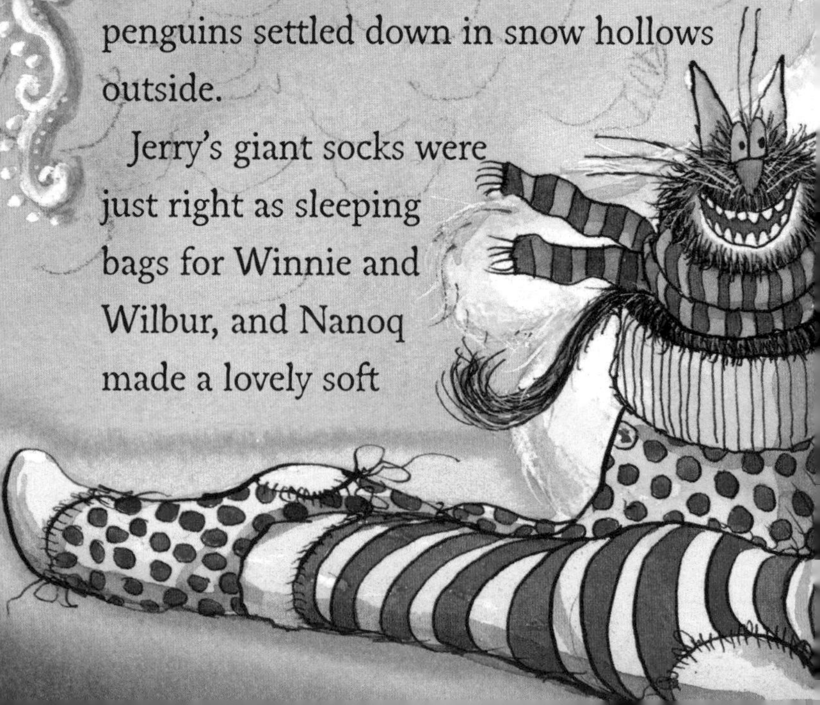

Jerry's giant socks were just right as sleeping bags for Winnie and Wilbur, and Nanoq made a lovely soft pillow to rest their heads on. Winnie read a joke from the joke book to make them all happy before they went to sleep.

'What did one snowman say to the other snowman?'

'Mrrow,' Wilbur didn't know.

'He said, "Can you smell carrots?" Hee hee,' laughed Winnie.

The spicy smell of gingerbread was stronger than the smell of Jerry's feet, and soon they were fast asleep.

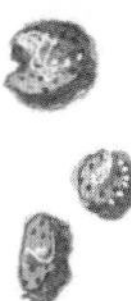

CHAPTER 8

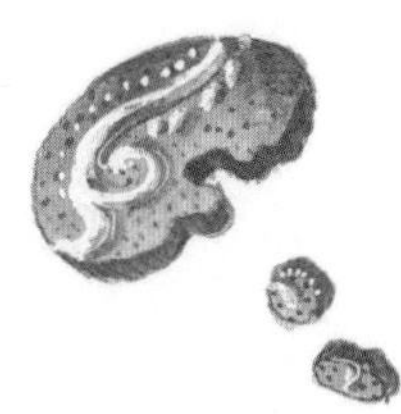

POLE TO POLE

Clunk!

A chunk of gingerbread wall landed on Winnie's head and woke her up.

'What in the whoopsy world is happening?' she said, sitting up in her sock sleeping bag.

Peck, peck, peck, crump!

'Those blooming penguins are eating our house!'

A whole gingerbread wall gave way.

'Is it morning? Are we going to find my family?' said Nanoq, absentmindedly chewing a chunk of wall.

'Never mind bears,' said Winnie. 'Look! It's Christmas Eve already, so we've got to find Santa fast!'

Wilbur tapped furiously at his PawTech and held it out for Winnie. It showed a picture map of the world. There was a polar bear at the North Pole and a penguin at the South Pole.

‘That’s as odd as a carrot in a pea pod!’ said Winnie. ‘We’ve got penguins all around us. Uh oh, we’re at the wrong Pole, aren’t we!’

‘Is that why my bears aren’t here?’ said Nanoq.

‘Meow,’ nodded Wilbur.

Winnie threw herself down on the snow.

‘Oh, no, oh woe! Our plan has all gone as wrong as a worm in a shoe shop! We’ve lost or opened or eaten all the presents for Santa, and now we're on the wrong side of the world to even wish him a Happy Christmas! Oh, woe, oh, woe, we're stuck in the snow!'

Wilbur pointed to the ski-doodle-doo broomstick.

'It's just not fast enough or strong enough, Wilbur!' said Winnie. Then she smiled, put her hat back on, and jumped to her feet. 'But I have got a clever-as-a-cockroach-with-a-calculator idea! We *will* get to Santa in time for Christmas.'

Winnie got bossy. 'Hold paws, you two,' she told Wilbur and Nanoq. 'No, not you, you penguins! You belong here. Winnie held Wilbur's other paw with one hand, and her broomstick with the other hand. 'Hold tight,' she said. 'I'm going to do *double* magic! When I say the word, "hup", we all jump. Everything will slow right down to tortoise-treacle speed for us, but the world will spin as fast as a firework under us. Right? Are we ready? Are we steady?' Wilbur and Nanoq nodded nervously.

Winnie raised her wand. 'One, two, three—Hup!' she shouted. She swished her wand one way, then the other. '**Abracadabra! Abracadabra!**' she shouted as they jumped into the air, and the world spun under them.

The strong magic from Winnie's wand fell in frozen sparkles that tinkled around them, as a whooshing blur of white, then blue and green, then white again rushed under their feet as they landed in the snow.

'Oo, I'm as dizzy as a fuzzy bee that's spun on a roundabout!' said Winnie. 'Look at that big lump of snow that's moving towards us! Oh, no, it's not snow, it's . . .'

'A bear!' said Nanoq. 'My family!'

And suddenly Winnie and Wilbur had to skip out of the way of gigantic hairy white bear hugs happening all around them.

'Well, that's a happy ending for you, Nanoq,' said Winnie. 'But I *still* can't see Santa, and we should at least go and say Happy Christmas to him now we're so near.'

'We know where Santa lives,' said one of the polar bears. 'We can take you there.'

'Oh, thank you!' said Winnie, as she climbed onto a big bear's back. Wilbur climbed onto Nanoq's back.

'Now, quick as you can, please cheesy-knees, take us to Santa!' said Winnie. Galloping on the back of a bear is a strange soft rocking-horse kind of a ride. Suddenly Winnie spotted Santa's house. 'Over there!' she squealed. But then she looked up. 'Oh, no. Is that dot in the sky Santa's sleigh flying away?'

90

'Meow,' confirmed Wilbur.

'Oh, no. We are too late!' wailed Winnie. She slid to the ground from her polar bear, and adjusted her hat which kept going wonky on her head. 'Oh, that's it, then. We haven't brought a happy Christmas to Santa at all. And we're ever such a long way from home.'

Wilbur was shivering and Winnie's nose was running. Both of them were hungry and thirsty and tired.

'Perhaps we can go and warm up in Santa's house even though he's not at home,' said Winnie. So she and Wilbur waved goodbye to Nanoq and her family, then they pushed at Santa's door which opened easily and wide.

CHAPTER 9

EVERYTHING SORTED FOR SANTA

There were six little elves inside, just on the other side of Santa's door.

'Happy Christmas!' they said.

'Goodbye,' they said.

'Oh,' said Winnie, 'we've only just arrived!'

'Yes, but we're just leaving,' said the elves. 'We're going home to our elf mummies and daddies and grannies and grandads and cousins and aunties and uncles and friends. Everyone should be home for Christmas!'

'Meow,' agreed Wilbur rather sadly.

Winnie could see now that the elves were just pulling on boots and hats, ready to go.

'But we're cold and tired!' said Winnie. 'And we've had enough of journeys.'

'Then you stay here and warm up,' said the elves. 'Santa won't mind.'

'Thank you!' said Winnie. 'And Happy Christmas!' She waved her wand. '**Abracadabra!**' A shower of sweets fell from the sky, and the elves caught them in their hats.

'Thank you, Winnie and Wilbur! Happy Christmas to you, too!'

And then they were gone.

Winnie and Wilbur shut Santa's door, and looked around.

'Oh, deary-slug-dumpling me, what a mess!' said Winnie. 'Santa's house makes my home seem tidy! He must have been running late and left in a rush with no time to put everything away. He'll come home as worn out as a tired turkey, and there's not even a chair he can sit his big red bottom on.'

'Meow?' suggested Wilbur, pointing at some little curly-toed elf boots.

'Good idea, that cat!' said Winnie. 'You and I can be tidy-up elves to tidy Santa's home. That can be our present to him, now that all the wrapped-up proper ones have gone. Where's my wand?' Winnie waved her wand. '**Abracadabra!**' And instantly she and Wilbur were in belted tunics and elf boots. 'Let's get to work!'

Wilbur sorted and stacked. Winnie swept with her broomstick.

'That's a bit better,' said

Winnie. 'But still not very Christmassy, is it? Shall we decorate it?'

'Mmmeow,' Wilbur nodded.

So Winnie waved her wand.

'**Abracadabra!**' And the piles of letters and pictures that children had sent to Santa were suddenly bunting strung all over the house. They put their advent calendar on Santa's mantelpiece.

'Now you, Broomy, are going to be the star of this Christmas show!' said Winnie, and with a swish of her wand, Winnie's broomstick sprouted into a handsome big Christmas tree.

'Abracadabra!'

The tree was festooned with brightly coloured lights, glittery tinsel, and shiny berry baubles. 'As beautiful as . . .

well, as beautiful as the spirit of Christmas!' said Winnie. 'Oh, won't Santa get a lovely surprise when he walks in!'

They put Santa's boot remover and slippers ready by the door for when he got home. They put his dressing gown on the peg by the door so that he could put it on as soon as he took his suit off. They plumped cushions on the chairs. They made a pan of steaming hot chocolate and a got a big mug and a supply of marshmallows ready for him.

Then they waited for him to come home.

And waited.

And waited.

'Meow,' pointed out Wilbur. He'd spotted a list on Santa's desk.

'Oo, is that the list of who is getting what presents?' said Winnie. 'Let's have a sneaky-peaky little look-see! Mrs

Parmar is getting a new tea cosy. Oh, she'll like that. And Jerry is getting new socks. That's just right, since he gave us two of his old ones. Clever old Santa! And the little ordinaries are getting all sorts. I wonder what . . .' She began to look through the list to peep at what presents were beside her and Wilbur's names, but Wilbur sternly smacked the list down again.

'Oh, I suppose it *would* spoil the surprise,' said Winnie. Then she sighed. 'But actually-pactually, I don't think we are going to get anything tonight, Wilbur, because we're not at home where Santa thinks we are.' She suddenly felt sad. And tired. She yawned a big yawn. 'I think it's time for sleep,' she said. 'I'm sure we'll wake up when Santa gets in.'

Winnie changed into her nightie. Then she settled into Santa's big chair by the fire, and she and Wilbur slept.

CHAPTER 10
MAGIC MOMENTS

Crump!

'What was that?' Winnie and Wilbur woke with a start.

Clomp-clomp!

'Oo, my giddy-goat-goodness!' said Winnie. 'I think that must have been Santa's sleigh landing, and now he's walking his big boots towards the door. Quick, I've got to get dressed!' Winnie snatched up her tights, and tried to pull them on.

'Ooer! My tights are full of something that isn't my legs!' she said.

'Meow!' said Wilbur, doing a happy dance. 'Meow, meow, meow!'

'Oo, you're right-as-a-shoe-that-isn't-a-left-one, Wilbur!' said Winnie. 'My tights are full of presents! Lovely Santa *did* bring us presents after all, one leg for you and one for me. What have we got?'

They pulled out present after present.

'Bat hair clips!' said Winnie. 'Just what I wanted. Oh, and what in the world? I've got goggles, Wilbur! Why did Santa give me goggles?'

Wilbur had a strange hat as well as the presents he'd asked for.

'Look, it's Santa Claus!
Oh, oh, oh, he's here, Wilbur!'

'Ho ho ho!' laughed Santa. 'Did I make you jump? Ho ho!'

'You did!' said Winnie. 'Oh, Santa, thank you from my mistle-toes to the top of my hat for all the presents!'

'Oh, Santa, we wanted to give *you* presents too, but, well, they've all got lost or eaten or given away on our journey here.'

'Oh, dear,' said Santa. 'But, actually, I've seen enough presents for a while. What I really want more than anything after working so hard to get the right presents to the right people at the right time, is . . .'

'. . . what?' said Winnie. 'I know, you'd like a big breakfast! Shall I rustle one up for you?'

'No, ho ho, nothing at all to eat, thank you, my friends,' said Santa. 'What I want is to play! I never have anyone to play with on Christmas Day. Will you two play with me, please?'

'Yippee!' said Winnie. 'Let's go outside and play in the snow now!'

So that's what they did. They made a snow Santa with a Winnie nose and Wilbur tail.

Wheee-crump!

They slid along the ice. They threw snowballs.

Splat!

Winnie waved her wand.

'Abracadabra!' and suddenly there were snowballs flying all over the place.

Duck! Catch! Splot!

'Ho ho, this is fun!' laughed Santa. 'But now I am a bit peckish. Let's go inside and eat.'

Santa made oozy cheese on toast with cranberry jelly.

'Shall we have some candied spiders as a topping?' suggested Winnie.

'Ho ho, no, not for me!' said Santa.

And, actually, when Winnie ate hers with no toppings at all, it was delicious. 'Yum! This toast is as beetle-much crunchy and the cheese is as oozy as gooey mashed-maggot jelly!' she said.

'Mrrow,' purred Wilbur, licking his lips.

After that, they were too full to move. They snuggled by the fire. And Wilbur had a nice idea.

'Meow?' he held up his PawTech.

'What's this?' said Santa.

Wilbur tapped on it and, as if by magic, there were all the funny times from Winnie and Wilbur's journey to Santa. Wilbur had been filming it all! And now he had added a jolly, jingly soundtrack.

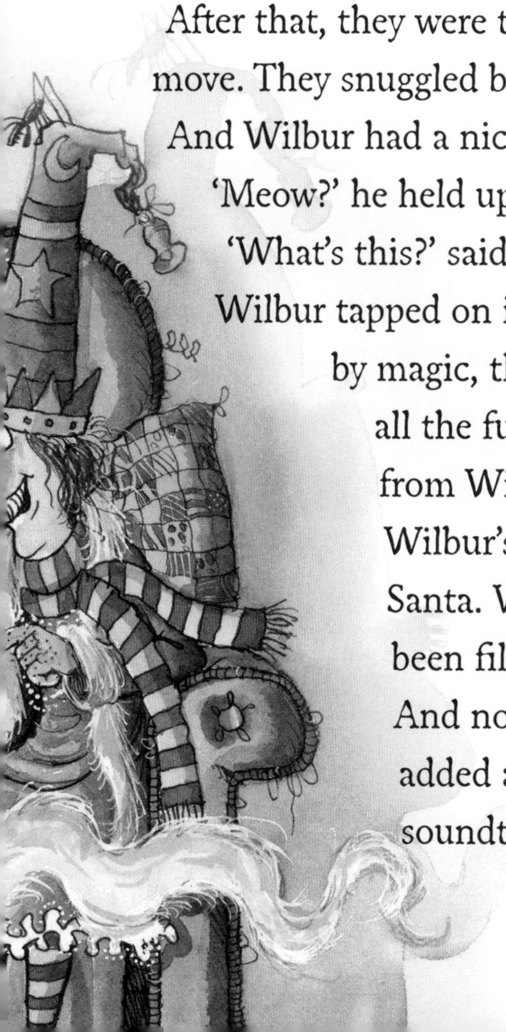

'Ho ho ho!' laughed Santa as he watched the gingerbread house collapse over Winnie and Wilbur and Nanoq. 'That's the funniest thing! Ho ho ho!'

'It wasn't that funny,' said Winnie. But, actually, looking at it now as a film, it was. 'Hee hee!' she was soon laughing too. Wilbur was giggling . . . and so was someone else. Or at least they were 'peep-peeping'.

'What in the whoopsy world was that?' said Winnie. 'Santa, did you say "peep peep"?'

'No, ho ho, I didn't!' said Santa.

'Meow,' Wilbur pointed up at Winnie's hat.

'Don't be silly, Wilbur,' said Winnie, 'hats don't *peep!*' She took off her hat.

'Oh!'

Because inside was one very small penguin.

'All the way from the South Pole!' said Winnie. 'How ever are we going to get him back there?'

But the little penguin seemed quite at home in Santa's house. He was nuzzling Santa's beard, and looking up at him with love.

'Peep peep!'

'Oh, that's as sweet as the first bleat of a baby lamb, that is!' said Winnie. 'You two are just like Wilbur and me!'

'Mrrhuff,' said Wilbur, who didn't often look dotingly on Winnie, even though he loved her dearly. But he looked at her now, and they both had the same thought at the same moment.

'Let's go home now, shall we?' said Winnie.

CHAPTER 11

HOME SWEET HOME

'Santa, please could Wilbur and I use your Christmas tree?' asked Winnie. 'It is actually my broomstick, you see, and we need it for getting us home.'

'Ho ho, home is where we should all be on Christmas Day,' said Santa. 'Of course you can use it. Thank you, thank you, for making my home so welcoming, for playing with me, for making me laugh, and for giving me a new little friend.

What wonderful presents!'

'You're very welcome, your Santa-ness!' said Winnie.

Winnie and Wilbur pulled the Christmas tree outside. They loaded it with bags of their stocking presents. Then Winnie laughed. 'Santa *knew* all along that we were going to fly away! That's why he gave us the goggles and the helmet, Wilbur.'

'Meow,' agreed Wilbur, fastening the strap.

'Do you know what, Santa?' said Winnie. 'I reckon you're even more magical than I am!'

Winnie and Wilbur sat in the Christmas tree branches, and Winnie waved her wand. '**Abracadabra!**'

Vrrrrrrrrrr!

The Christmas tree rocket rose up.

Winnie waved her wand again, over Santa's house below. 'Abracadabra!' Suddenly the reindeer in their pen had decorated antlers, and Santa was dressed in a penguin onesie and flipper slippers.

'Ho ho!'

'Peep peep!'

'Off we go, with a ho ho ho!' said Winnie, pointing her wand up into the sky. 'Goodbye, Santa! Happy Christmas!'

Zooom!

They rocketed over ice and land and sea towards home. They were so fast that the coloured lights on their tree rocket blurred and shone like glimmering Northern Lights above Winnie's house below. Jerry, Scruff, Mrs Parmar, and lots of little ordinaries rushed outside to greet them.

Crump!

The Christmas tree rocket landed.

'Hooray!' shouted all their friends. 'Welcome home, Winnie and Wilbur!'

Everyone wanted to hear about Winnie and Wilbur's adventure. So Wilbur linked his PawTech to a big screen and everyone settled down to watch his film.

'You got a *real* teddy!' said the little girl.

'So are my old socks still at the South Pole?' laughed Jerry.

'And now I've got a Christmas present for all of you,' said Winnie. 'Who wants a ride on the Christmas tree rocket?'

The first person to put her hand up was Mrs Parmar!

Whoosh!

Up went Winnie and Wilbur and Mrs Parmar.

'Oh, this is marvellous!' said Mrs Parmar. She was wearing a flying jacket that Santa had put in her stocking, almost as if he'd known that she was going to go flying . . .

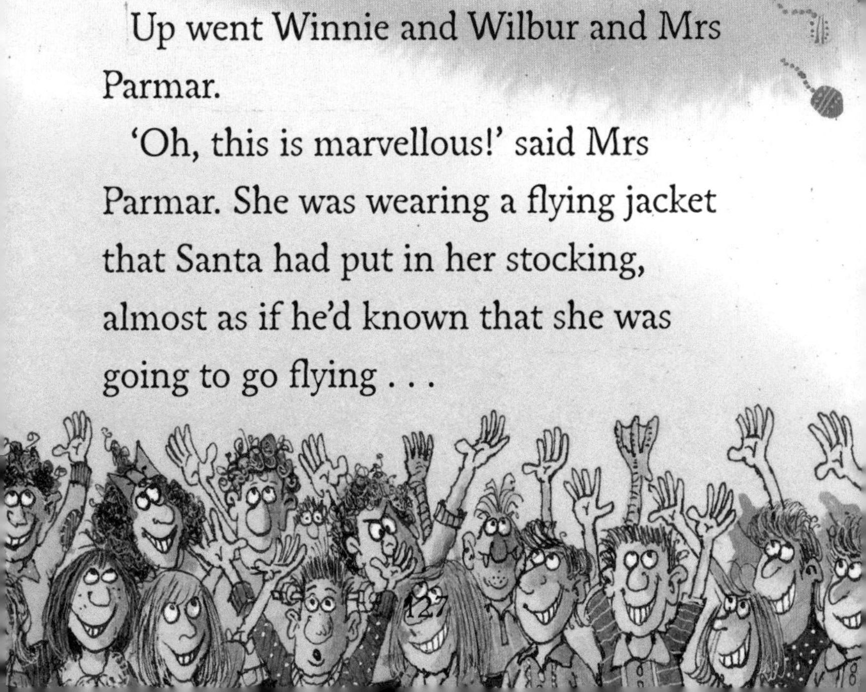

And while they were up high in the sky, Winnie waved her wand, 'Abracadabra!' to make it snow marshmallows on all her friends below.

'Happy Christmas, everyone and everytwo and everythree and to Wilbur and to me!' said Winnie.